The Street Girl Who Stole an Executive's Heart

A touching story of pain, betrayal, love and

acceptance

BOOK 1

O. JOHNS

TABLE OF CONTENTS

CHAPTER 1

*"L*aura! Laura! Open this door!" Norah *shouted from the other side of the locked door as fear and a sense of helplessness engulfed her whole being. She could hear her fourteen-year-old daughter Laura's faint scream coming from her bedroom sounding as if someone was covering her mouth. For almost twenty minutes, her mind froze as she stood outside the door while hearing shuffling movements and sobs coming out of the room.*

Prior to her remarriage, Norah was an outgoing 32-year-old woman working as a concierge in one of the top hotels in the sprawling city of Suntan. About a year before she met Mike, a 36-year-old janitor at the local high school, Norah had the misfortune of losing her husband Derick, the father to her beloved Laura to Leukemia. She found it difficult to raise her daughter alone as a single parent. It was not long after Derick's death that Norah ran into Mike at a potluck, organized by one of her friends. They got along almost instantly and soon Mike; a short-tempered stout man became a permanent fixture at Norah's apartment. They got married within a year of their meeting.

Four years into their marriage, Norah became a shadow of herself. She lost her attractiveness, her spark and preferred solitary life to the vibrant life she once had before she met Mike. He became so intolerant and physically abusive to her and her young daughter Laura. It has been nine months now since Mike lost his job. The local school board fired him for gross misconduct. Since then, he has resorted to heavy drinking and coming home past midnight. On this night, he came back from his drinking spree and went straight into Laura's room. He locked the door behind him, removed his pants and was suddenly on top of the young defenseless Laura who was deep asleep, clutching a teddy bear to her chest.

"Good afternoon Mr. Jones", said his personal assistant Janice as Brian Jones the C.E.O of the renowned Data Integrated Software Corporation stepped into the office. At six feet two inches, Brian is good looking in a rugged way. His light blue eyes, gentle voice and warm disposition makes him the target of most women, even the married ones. His sharp sense of dressing can be deceiving because

beneath all the glamour is a very intelligent man who knows his onions about his job.

By circumstances, Brian came back to work much earlier than he had wanted to. The loss of his wife Hellen and daughter Janet from an automobile accident, twenty-four months ago continue to weigh him down. The effect of their sudden deaths still has an impact on the business as well as the public community of the city of Vancouver.

"Good day to you too" replied Mr. Jones. Ever since that fateful day, Brian has literally been a walking spaced Zombie in mourning, barely noticing people, including the beautiful personal assistant who has served him with diligence and dedication all through it. She is almost at her wits end, frustrated by the seemingly wait, for her handsome boss to make the first move.

Brian and Hellen were high school sweethearts and had been inseparable since their prom night. They both went to Harvard, with Hellen at the medical school and Brian, the mechanical engineering school. They excelled exceptionally in their individual academic pursuit, going on to work on doctorate degrees. Hellen became the Director of Pediatrics at the Research Centre of the Public Health Ministry of the City of Vancouver. Brian on the other hand founded the

Data Integrated Software Corporation. A company credited for revolutionizing digital concepts of social media beyond what one would have comprehended a decade ago. Hellen and Brian married eight years ago, and a year later had a baby girl; they named her Janet. She became the center of their existence and brought so much joy into their lives. All of that ended when Hellen and Janet died in a motor accident. Hellen was thirty-one, a few months younger than Brian was.

After comfortably seating in his chair, Brian started perusing his notes, making sure he had covered all that was required of him for the day schedule. He suddenly felt the urge to get some latte from the Starbuck café across the street from his office. He crossed the road and a few metres before he got to the door to the café, he noticed a young beautiful, though haggard looking woman walking toward his direction. She was pushing a shopping cart. He entered the shop and the first thing he noticed, was a middle-aged couple snuggling and cuddling at a corner, very oblivious to anything around them. They appeared engulfed in a world of their own. Brian did not make much of it. He proceeded straight to the counter and ordered for what he wanted and added, a couple of croissants. He picked up his order and moved to sit adjacent to the couple who continued with their public display of affection. He sat down, and was about to take the first seep of the latte, when suddenly, like a bolt from the blue, it hit him.

All the pent up emotions that had been building up inside him since Hellen died, came rushing to the surface. Suddenly his eyes swelled up with tears that came out gently and without provocation. He abandoned his snack, rushed for the door, and left the shop. He drove straight away to the grave of his wife and daughter after picking up a bouquet of roses from a store on the way. He longed dearly to be in the company of his beloved Hellen and their departed daughter Janet. He has made it a habit to come here every Thursday afternoon but the excruciating pain that he feels each time he visits never recedes.

He spent almost an hour by their side, talking to each one of them separately while recollecting and remembering Hellen's smiles and their daughters nagging questions about almost everything she saw. How precious those moments were and he wondered if he could ever feel that way again in this lifetime. He departed from the graveside and went home to the now lonesome humongous bloated aristocratic mansion, which sits on a hilltop, with a bird's view of the city. Somehow, he felt so lonely and lost being in this big house by himself. It was not supposed to be this way. He and Hellen had planned to fill this place with the laughter of children. Now he dread coming to this empty house.

The house that Brian and Hellen built is a remarkable sight. It has Front split parlors with two living rooms-furnished with golden sofas. Two dining rooms – small and large, both with exquisite dining sets, beautiful golden Persian chandeliers hang above them. Endowing the family room are pictures of their families going back two generations. To keep up with the culinary trend, the mansion has an expansive Kitchen that is equipped with all sorts of gadgets as well as a well-stocked pantry. It also has a large study, an IT tech security room, a conservatory or music room, six bathrooms, a great hall, a large library, a pool house w/ indoor-outdoor pool and six bedrooms. As he entered his house, he considered calling one of his workers but thought against it. He took off his shoes and went to the liquor cabinet. He fetched a bottle of rum and a coke, got himself a glass, added a few cubes of ice, poured out a drink and sat on a sofa. He took his drink quietly while recollecting the events of the day, unable to understand what came over him at the Cafe. After downing the entire bottle, he staggered to his bedroom, which was upstairs and passed out. He woke up from his drunken slumber at the sound of his alarm clock in the morning.

CHAPTER 2

en years ago, Laura left home after that traumatic encounter with her stepfather Mike. He had violated her and taken her innocence in the most brutal way imaginable. She ran away from home a few weeks after that ugly night when her mother seemed reluctant to press charges against Mike for what he had done to her. Laura could no longer trust her mother as she finally realized she was alone with no one to protect her even within her own home. The night she left, she took the only possession that gave her comfort, the small teddy bear, which her late father had given her on her 7th birthday. She fled home not knowing where to go. The only certainty on her mind was the need to get as far away as possible from her mother and Mike. She hopped into a bus that took her to the city center and prayed to find refuge in some corner of the sprawling buildings of the city. Laura convinced herself that any semblance of safety would be enough for her. She became aware that from this moment she has to fend for herself without relying on anybody.

Forced into adulthood by circumstances at the age of fourteen Laura did whatever it took to survive city street life. Two years after leaving home and moving from one shelter to another in search of bed space, Laura met Anthony, a twenty-six-year-old Afghan war veteran who was also living on the streets and blessed with a gift and a passion for sculpting. Anthony could sculpt almost anything if he put his mind to it. He had a way of making an object come to life with his sculpting techniques. The thing he lacked was the application of this gift for better use. "Tony," as they called him on the streets decided to take Laura under his wings and became her mentor, defender and protector.

Laura became Tony's understudy, watching and learning from him the principles and concepts behind art as a discipline. She absorbed his teachings quickly, and started applying them to her own art but using her own expressions. Many people found her work revolutionary. She soon started displaying her sculpts on her mobile shopping cart, moving from street to street and finding buyers for them. Taking stock of her environment and vowing to make something out of her life, Laura started saving from the sale of her work with the plan that she would one day rent her own place and have a gallery where she can display and sell her own collections. It did not take Laura long to get an abandoned shack, which she turned into a livable place and a quasi-gallery of artifacts. However, it lacked so many things, which were of considerable importance. Necessities such as running water and toilet facilities were top on the list. At best, her shack had a living room, and a bedroom. The rest of the amenities she hoped to get whenever she could. Regardless, she finally had a place she could call home and her own.

When Brian Jones woke up, he only had a faint recollection of the previous day's event. He decided to go out that morning to get his coffee believing it would clear his head as well as his thoughts. He drove out to his favorite café not far away from the company's head office, located on the main thoroughfare boulevard at 1330 Albert Street in the city of Vancouver. He parked his car a few minutes' walk from the shop, and just as he turned away after closing his car door to go inside, he crashes into a shopping cart full of sculptures and artifacts, pushed by a young beautiful woman.

"You people should look where you go," retorted the young woman pushing the cart.

"If you think I am going to say sorry to you, then you have something else coming. Who do you think you are, eh?" the woman shouted as she wheeled her cart away.

Before Brian could respond, the woman had disappeared around the corner. Brian was in a lot of pain, stunned and in discomfort. The only evidence, which suggested something had happened, was a small teddy bear on the ground. The teddy bear had apparently fallen from the shopping cart that ran into him. He tried to get the woman's attention by shouting after her but she was far-gone.

Dusting himself and picking up the teddy bear off the ground, Brian went on to get his coffee. He picked up a cup and went to his office. He began preparing notes for the conference call he had scheduled with his counterpart in Tokyo. As much as he tried to focus on his preparation, he found his mind drifting to his encounter with the woman earlier on. He called in his secretary and instructed her, to place a call to Tokyo and reschedule the meeting, because he was not feeling well. His phone rang and the Vice President of sales division, Beth asked for an audience with him. Beth went in holding some files but sensed immediately, that her boss was not his usual self.

Occasionally, they would joke and even one time, tried to go out on a date after Hellen was gone, but there was no spark. She told him she had some numbers, she wanted him to look at but that can wait until an appropriate time. Mr. Jones agrees and admit to her that his head is not in the right place that morning. On her way out, she teases him, suggesting that he probably needs a woman's touch to take away all his worries and tension. Beth reminds him of the good things he is missing, and offers to come back and give him a shoulder massage because, as she puts it, he looked tense. Mr. Jones reminded her of the office protocol, how it would be improper, and thanked her for her concern for his welfare. Beth looked a bit embarrassed and left his office mumbling some incoherent words to herself.

Immediately Beth left his office, Brian, as a matter of urgency, took out from his pocket a small bottle of anti-anxiety drugs with the clear intention of taking two capsules as usual, to calm himself down. Just as he was about to take the capsules, he found his mind drifting back to the encounter with the shopping cart woman whose teddy bear, he had in his drawer. He wondered how he would find her to return her teddy. He left his office driving in a very apprehensive mood. Barely ten minutes into his journey, had he seen a woman who was sculpting by the street sidewalk? As he drove closer, he became certain she was the one he was looking for. The problem for Brian then was finding a big enough parking spot for the Toyota Cruiser he was driving. He was anxious to find a location close to where the woman was, and in the process forgot to pay attention to what was happening on the road. Suddenly there was a thud and the sound of breaking glasses as his vehicle came to a screeching stop. Brian had hit the vehicle in front of him, smashing its taillights. Before his mind could process what had happened, the angry driver of the other vehicle was by his window banging it, and demanding he come out. He did and after arguing for a few minutes, they both agreed to move their vehicles out of the road to the roadside where they could settle the issue.

By the time all the fracas involving this minor accident was finished, Brian raced up on foot to find the woman but he was too late. The shopping cart woman had vanished. He asked around if anybody knew where the woman lived and got no positive response. One of the people hanging around was Tony, the self- defender and protector of Laura who saw an opportunity of making some quick buck. He approached Brian and offered to give him the information *he sought after, but for a price. Brian took out a twenty-dollar bill and pressed it into Tony's hand expecting the information to flow but Tony just mumbled to himself and says nothing. In desperation, Brian adds another bill of twenty but that too did not produce any result. "Where are you from?" Brian asked the man. As he, turns away disappointed and in disgust to leave, Tony offers to locate the woman for him on the condition that he comes back the next day and tells him he is Puerto Rican.*

Brian heads to his car, opens the door and sits wondering whether his behavior was normal. Meanwhile, no sooner had Brian left that location, Tony slipped into the back alley where Laura was scavenging trash bins, looking for any thrown away artifacts. He informed her of the development with the man looking for her. A few minutes later, while still sitting in his car and trying to assess his own behavior, he sees Tony and the shopping cart woman emerge from an alley talking, and then go their separate ways. Brian decides to follow her to find out where she was going and most probably find out where she lives. Brian gave himself a considerable distance from the woman pushing the cart, making sure he did not blow his cover. He drives slowly. Thirty minutes into his drive while following the woman, he notices he is driving out of the city into a poor dilapidated suburban neighborhood. Suddenly the woman stops and turns to her right to a white painted house and disappears into it. Brian slowly parks his car some distance from the house, fetches out the teddy bear and approaches the house to return the lost item to its rightful owner.

He knocked at the door twice before the woman came to find out who it was. She opens the door, sees and recognize the man who bumped into her cart and probably is responsible for the loss of her best friend "Lilly" the teddy bear. He stands at her door, with "Lilly" clutched to his chest and expecting an invitation. Instead, she grabs the teddy, and asks him to leave. Brian is surprised at her hostility, and as he leaves, wonders if this woman is aware of the trouble he had to go through to find her. He got back into his car and drove straight home where he helped himself to a glass of wine, made a sandwich and went to the tech security room to work on his project. He finished working within a few hours, took a swim and had diner then retired to his bedroom.

The next day, after Brian had settled down to work for a few hours in his expansive office at the headquarters, he begun to contemplate whether to go and visit the shopping cart woman. He prayed he would find her at the same place he saw her the previous day. He arrived there shortly before midday and found her sculpting and looking quite a mess. Her hair was disheveled and she wore a dirty overall, covered with all sorts of colors. The socks on her feet were a mismatch, and her face had paint all over. Brian wondered if this was some ritual with sculptors or they were just plane too lazy to bother about their looks. He greeted her and reminded her who he was. He asked if she could spare a few minutes of her time to have lunch with him at the restaurant across on Nathan Street. She declined the invitation at first, but changed her mind and agreed to have lunch, just to get rid of him.

"What do you want from me?" She asked him as they walk towards the restaurant.

"I do not know but what I know is I am famished and would be privileged to have your company" Brian responded.

Laura could not believe what this stranger was saying.

"How would you want to be in my company, yet you don't know me?" Is this how people of your class collect women to go sleep with?" She asked angrily.

"Oh! No," Brian protested. "Please! That is not what this is all about I am doing this because I owe you."

"What do you owe me? Are you mocking me or something?" She asked looking serious.

Brian tried to explain what he meant. He told her he owed her an apology for keeping her teddy for as long as he did. He believed she must have been devastated thinking she had lost it. They entered the restaurant and the waiter who seemed to know Laura very well, led them, to their table. As they walked towards their table, it was evidently clear that they were drawing attention to themselves in a negative way of almost everyone in the room. Brian decided to ignore their glances and proceeded to the table, pulled out a chair for his companion and they both sat and ordered for their meals. No sooner had the waiter taken the orders; Laura pulled out a joint and lit it right inside the restaurant, she took a puff and exhaled the smoke towards Brian. Realizing what was about to happen, Brian jumped out of his seat snatched the joint from her hands and put it out, before the smell could affect the room. He then settled back to his seat. In retaliation, Laura kicks him quite hard on the foot, leaving him grimacing with pain all over his face. As if that is not enough, Laura who is keen on humiliating him some more, chooses the time when she sees the waiter heading to their table with their food, to carry out her revenge. She silently takes off her shoes, extends her foot to Brian's crotches; and begin to massage his balls with her toes. Brian's first impulse is to shout but he holds himself. He does not want to draw anyone's attention to what is going on under the table. Just as quickly as she had used her foot to attack his balls, she immediately withdrew the foot, as soon as the waiter was on her way back and acted as if nothing had happened. Brian was stunned at her audacity. They ate their meal in silence without uttering a word.

" Please forgive my manners, my name is Brian, what is yours," He asked her.

"I do not want to do names right now, let us just eat and go our separate ways" Laura said.

Brian was finding this beautiful but shabbily dressed woman interesting. He realizes that since Hellen's death, this is the first time he can remember enjoying himself, in the company of a woman and interestingly a woman whose name he is yet to find out. Brian convinces himself that this woman is beautiful and pleasurable to watch, as she gives a coolness and peace to his eyes, heart and mind.

After the meal, he pays the bill and they part ways, each wondering if they would ever meet again and do this one more time. Brian heads back to his office with a feeling he cannot describe but quite enjoys. The first person he runs into as he enters the building is Beth the Vice President of sales division, who immediately notices a change in the demeanor of her boss. She wondered if he had met someone wherever he was coming from.

CHAPTER 3

The next morning before going to work, Brian made up his mind to pass by the woman's house and say hello. He pulls over by the house, parks his car, and just as he was about to knock at the door she opens it.

"So what do you want this time?" she asks him

"Well, I was driving by and thought to stop by and say hello. May I come in?" He asks.

"You may, but first you need to tell me what you want from me at this time of the day," she says.

"Spend time with you, is that good enough or should I continue." He asks.

"I will let you in only because you look pathetic standing there in that suit" she replies.

Laura lets him in. Brian looks around the tiny room fascinated by the collection of art and artifacts. "Did you sculpt and collect all these?" He asks her.

"What do you think? You cannot see a woman like me doing all of this right?" She replies.

"That is not what I mean, I am just amazed you have all these and you are not sharing it with the world given how talented you really are." Brian says.

With a puzzled look on his face, he asks her "Who really are you?" Brian enquires.

It appears she heard only parts of his comments because of her response.

"Do you really mean it when you say am talented or is this a way of getting into my good books?" Laura wanted to know.

However, he avoids her question. "There is the smell of coffee in the air, are you brewing some?" Brian asks as he changes the topic.

"Yes, would you like a cup?" answered Laura

Laura pours out coffee into two mugs and hands him one while she keeps the other for herself and takes the seat opposite him. She brings out a rolled up joint. She lights it, inhales a few puffs, and offers it to Brian. He declines but instead offers Laura unsolicited advice about the effects of smoking and particularly marijuana.

Laura continues smoking her joint while understudying Brian and looking at him directly in the eyes. She finds him attractive and gentle, well-mannered and charming. She wonders why a man like him would find anything of interest in a woman of her repute. She gets up from her chair and sits on his lap blowing smoke right onto his face. Brian is startled but does not resist her move. She starts kissing him gently and he responds to her with subtle passion. Laura feels it right away like a bolt of lightning running down her spine. She digs for more holding tightly unto him as if her life depended on it when suddenly; Brian pulls away and apologizes to her for trying to take advantage of her. Laura is stunned. The men she had been with before never ran away whenever the opportunity arose.

"What kind of man is this, did he not find her attractive?" She wondered silently.

Brian excused himself and left for the office. Laura was frustrated and confused and began to question her own sanity. How could she feel this way and where did this feeling, the electricity that engulfed her entire body come from when Brian kissed her? She had never experienced such emotion with any man; the way she had a few minutes ago. She remembered the many times in her past, men who were much stronger forced themselves onto her; their ugly touches on her body and how her skin crawled each time it happened. She hated their breath and wondered if that was all, there was to it.

What really is the big deal with sex? If that is what they call making love, then love must be the biggest fraud ever. Given that, men took it by force whether she wanted it or not, did that also constitute making love? She wondered.

Nevertheless, what about this man. Why did it feel different when he kissed me? She pondered.

Rather than continue dwelling on issues she could not find answers to at that moment, Laura decided to change into her work clothes. She took out the dry brushes, the unfinished sculpts, and other items she had been working on the previous day, placed them in her shopping cart and wheeled herself to her station.

Brian Jones is not in his usual mental fortitude this morning as he drives to make his appointment with his counsellor, Dr. Andrew Sullivan, a psychologist. Brian is beginning to feel like a man who is on the verge of losing it. The woman with no name has me bewitched. Why did I go visit her in the first place? As streams, of emotions interrupted his thought.

"Oh! That kiss! What a sensation it was and that face, it was angelic," Brian muttered to himself.

As he entered the block housing the hospital and on his way to Dr. Sullivan office, he runs into the good doctor who was on his way to the hospital pharmacy to pick up some drugs for his wife. He invites Brian to join him for the walk to the pharmacy.

"You look a mess, you need to get a hold of yourself, Brian" said Dr. Sullivan. "Is everything okay?" He added.

"I do not want to talk about it here with you but I will wait for you in your office. I truly need your advice", said Brian.

"In that case, see you when I get back. Most probably in ten minutes" his counsellor said and left.

Brian entered the elevator, which took him to the fifth floor where Dr. Sullivan office is located. He went past the receptionist desk, went quietly into the doctor's office, and waited for him. When, Suzie, Dr. Sullivan's assistant walked into her boss's office, she was surprised to find Brian seated. "Mr. Jones, I am sorry, I did not know you were already here. The doctor left to pick up something downstairs and he should be back shortly." Suzie said.

"I know I ran into him on my way to your office and decided to wait here for him, if that is okay with you," says Brian.

"It is my pleasure to have you visit us Mr. Jones," Suzie said as she was leaving the room.

"How is your mom doing, tell her I truly enjoyed the apple pie she sent the other day." Brian told her.

"Most certainly, I will, she has been asking after you." Suzie told him as she left the room.

As he patiently waited for Dr. Sullivan, Brian started to go through different emotions. The most pressing of them were fear and excitement. Fear! That his feelings about the woman with no name was somehow a betrayal of Hellen's trust. Excitement! That he was experiencing a certain kind of vitality, an emergence of freshness within his soul, a newness. He was hopeful once again; at that moment, Dr. Sullivan walked in interrupting his train of thought and invites him into the private chambers.

"Come right in" Dr. Sullivan calls out as Brian walks in and sits down.

"How are you my friend?" Dr. Sullivan asks.

"So, so", Brian answered.

"What did you want to talk about? "Dr. Sullivan enquired.

"Well, it is a long story. You see, you are my doctor as well as my brother in-law, and that should make it easy for you to understand. You have known how Hellen and Janet's death has left me broken. Something has happened to me and I need to share it with you. I have been on a kind of rollercoaster of varying emotions these past few days."

Brian goes on to narrate his encounter with the woman with no name, his visit to her place and the extraordinary feelings she imprinted on him after their kiss.

"I am so confused; you won't believe I still don't know her name." Brian says.

"Well, that is a good start if I may say so, considering where you have been. The traumatic experience you have gone through after losing two members of your family at the same time is indescribable. What this tells me is that you have begun to heal from your mental and emotional wounds. Nevertheless, I would ask you to be cautious and move slowly. You mind me asking; what does she do for a living? Dr. Sullivan asked Brian.

"She is an artist, a very intriguing one. Very bold, beautiful and occasionally smokes pot." Brian tells him.

"Listen to me; I am going to tell you this as family not as your doctor. Anybody who smokes pot is trouble and most often than not, have a distorted worldview. My sister Hellen as you know was clean, because of that she had a purpose, and it is what enabled her, to achieve what she had *in the shortest time possible. I would like to see you with a person who matches your standard, both mentally and socially. Not a misfit who smokes pot. How sure are you that she is not after your money?" the good doctor asked. Brian could not believe what was coming out of his in-laws' mouth. He became speechless but thanked the doctor for his time. Shortly after, their chat ended and they both left the office, Brian headed home while Dr. Sullivan for the gym.*

The next morning, as Brian Jones woke up, the first thought that came to his mind was the need to deal with this crisis of the heart because it was slowly crippling his mental functions. He had to go and see that woman. He drove to her place and just as he was about to knock on the door, he realized it was open. He quietly pushed it and went in. He found her dancing to a reggae tune with her back to the door, her long golden hair swaying with every swing of her hips and upper body. Everything about her seemed synchronized and in harmony with her slim body and matching height. She was smoking a joint as she danced. It would seem she sensed some presence in the room because she suddenly turned. When she saw it was Brian, she shouted at him to get out.

"What do you want, please leave, I don't want to see you here again," she yells

"Please! Hear me out first and then I will leave" Brian replies.

"Say whatever it is you have to say and leave" Laura tells him

"It is about the last time I was here. I am sorry with the way I reacted. I have come to apologize. I know how I hurt you. Please forgive me". Brian said this with sadness in his eyes.

She takes one look at him and feels so much compassion for him.

"Please sit down. Would you like some coffee? I made it like the last time"

Brian sits down while Laura goes to fetch the coffee. She comes back, hand him his coffee and sits next to him on the couch. Laura wonders why she is not afraid to be alone with this man as she is with other men.

They talk about a number of things; coffee, artifacts, paintings, sculpting and marijuana. Then Laura asks him about what he enjoys doing for leisure. Brian finds this question hard to answer because he has had no social life since he lost his family. He told Laura, he had been busy with work and kind of lost touch with reality and thinks she can help him retrace his path. Laura felt relief and thrilled hearing him say that. She grins and lightens up at the obvious invitation by this man. She too, desperately wanted to be a part of his world regardless. She agrees on one condition. She would show him her world first. They shake hands on it. Laura then slips into the other room and changes into one of her comfortable dress, comes out and asks Brian if they could start their adventure right away. He agrees and off they went.

She directs Brian to the fancy side of town where rich people live; asks him to pull over by a street and park the car. He parks the car, they come out, and she leads him into an alley. She stops by a bin and informs Brian that most of the collection she saw him admire at her house have come from that bin. Laura starts rummaging through it. She brings out unbelievable items that the rich had thrown away. Expensive looking plates, cups, china dishes, cutleries and even Chinese food still neatly packed and secure in their delivery boxes. Fresh looking apples and oranges. Brian could not believe his eyes, he wondered though if all the items she had found would find their way into his car. He pushes the thought out of his mind because;

he had agreed to do this. Brian finds her delight so refreshing and intoxicating, in addition the innocent look on her face is priceless. Laura becomes giddier seeing Brian's amazement at her find. She felt a strong urge to rush and hug him for doing this with her. He helped gather her discovery and together they carried them into his car.

As they drove away, Brian suggested they go to the beach and find something to eat. Laura starts laughing and giggling a bit. "Did I say anything amusing?" he asked.

"No, I was just wondering why we should go and eat at a beach restaurant when we have our newly minted Chinese food with us. Don't you want to have some?" She was definitely teasing him.

They got to the beachfront parking lot, collected their parking ticket and head for the eatery front door. Laura excused herself to go to the lady's room while Brian goes to find a place to sit which had a good view of the open water. He waited for her so they could place their order. She emerges from the washroom looking quite stunning. Her blue colored eyes, so much accentuated by the blue eye shadow she had applied. Brian for the first time got a clear glimpse of her beauty. With her hair freely flowing and a little touch of lipstick on her lips, she indeed is remarkably beautiful with a touch of innocence as well, he thought. After the waiter takes their orders and leaves, Brian decides that he had enough of the suspense over her name.

"Do you know it feels like I have known you for a decade and still you have not told me your name?"

"Oh, That! Are you sure I have not told you my name?"

"I am truly sorry; my name is Laura and the rest you already know".

"Laura! That is a beautiful name and why should somebody stubborn have such a beautiful name while one who crashes into people; pushing a shopping cart named Brian?" He asked

Laura bursts out laughing and looking quite pleased with Brian.

"I did not know you are a comedian as well. Is it because they don't pay you well that you dabble into comedy?" She asked.

"Well, you know one has to be cautious and not put all ones' eggs into one basket," Brian replied. They both laughed as Brian took hold of Laura's hand and cuddled it in his. He moved closer to Laura and whispered into her ears. She giggled and in high spirits rewarded Brian with a kiss on his lips and chin. Whatever Brian had whispered,

must have worked some magic on her? Laura became alive from that moment on.

Their order arrived just in time as Brian was starting to become impatient because of the long wait. Laura had hash brown, three stripes of bacon, two sausages and two scramble eggs with a cup of coffee. Brian on the other hand, had three slices of toasted buttered bread, two bacon pieces and three poached eggs with coffee. They ate their food in silence but glancing at each other appreciatively.

The setting and atmosphere in the restaurant was ideal, especially for Laura who had never dined in such a fine environment. Knowing no other life but the hard one, she had accepted her lot a long time ago, because she did not see any other life for her. Inwardly, she began to overcome the apprehension she had at the beginning about Brian. She wondered why this fine, handsome and smart man is showing this much interest in an uneducated woman like her when there are so many women out there for him. As these thoughts were going through her mind, Brian made a call to his office. He cancelled all his appointments for the day and had them re-scheduled. He was determined to give Laura all his attention as long as she needed it this day.

They finished their meal and Brian suggested they go for a walk on the beach, enjoy the sun, as well as the cooling effect of the ocean breeze. Laura jumped at the idea with so much enthusiasm as if she had been waiting for him to ask.

Laura recalls seeing on television, couples walk on the beach holding hands and having so much fun with one another. She used to wonder if it was real or just fake. However, right now, at this moment, she realizes it is real. She is beginning to find, it is real with the man who does not seem to want give up on her. They get to the beach, take off their shoes and step onto the sand barefooted. Laura races to the water and kicks it towards Brian splashing his shirt and pants with water. She turns and runs in the opposite direction. He runs after her, catches up with her and they both fall down on the sand with Laura on top. For a moment, they just stare at each other with their noses rubbing, the passion in their eyes evident. Laura kisses him on the lips and Brian opens his mouth to receive, she goes for the jugular ferociously by plunging her tongue deep into Brian's reservoir of emotion. He reciprocates as well. Using the tongue as her new weapon instead of her foot like on previous occasion, her tongue searches for Brian's plains and valleys. She discover the right spot where her fire feels quenched. She lingers there as if for eternity. Laura wishes she could live there forever.

They remain in the state where their tongues did the talking for about two minutes until someone flipped some sand over their heads. It was a young boy running nearby and playing with a dog. They stopped what they were doing, raised their heads and saw some people watching them. They simultaneously burst out laughing. They got on their feet and Brian suddenly carries her and runs into the water. He stops midway into the water and threatens to throw her into it. Laura begs for mercy and promises to do and be anything he wants her to be if he does not follow through with his threat. He takes her back to dry land and insists that she puts her promises down in writing.

"What promises?" Laura quips, "I was under duress and thus the promises do not count"

"Oh! Really, you want us to do it again, until I get what is due to me. This time I am going to get a witness." Brian says, as he tries to scoop her back into his hands.

Laura did not wait for Brian to reach her. She took off towards the parking lot and waited for him by the car.

"I have never seen anybody as crazy as you are. You are simply nuts!" She tells him when he catches up with her at the parking lot where she was waiting for him.

"Brian, do you mind if we go back to my place?" she asks.

"Sure, did you forget to pick up something or what?" He enquired.

He opens the passenger side door of the car for her. She gets into the car and starts to cry silently. Suddenly, the cry turns to a loud sob. Startled, Brian rushes to the driver's side of the car, gets in and pulls her gently towards him holding her tightly stroking her curled hair.

"Did I say or do anything to upset you?" He asks her.

"No! No! It is not you. I am sorry am ruining the day," she said.

"Would you like to talk about it?" He asks her.

Laura avoids responding directly to his question. Instead, she asks him if he likes her. He responds in the affirmative.

"If you do like me, why have you not asked me about who I really am and where I come from?" Laura asks

Brian was silent for a while before responding to her question. "You see Laura; experience has taught me not to rush people. Therefore, I have chosen not to impose myself onto things that are quite personal to you. I wanted you, on your own volition to offer that information at your own convenience without feeling coerced. Secondly, I am not going anywhere. This means I am going to be here. There is a lot of time, to get to know you. In addition, it is my desire that when you feel comfortable with me you will tell me whatever you think I should know. What I am trying to say is, I enjoy having you around me and I will know everything about you when the time is right and when you want me to know.

"But, if you don't ask me, how will I tell you about it?" Laura asked.

"Don't misunderstand me by thinking that I will not ask, of course I will. What I am saying is, when you feel comfortable enough with me, and I happen to ask you about almost anything; you can choose to withhold or give information freely from your heart because of the trust you have in me. I would hate to make you feel pressured because of my need".

"So are we good on this?" Brian asks Laura

"Yes we are, I now beginning to understand." She assures him.

"Do you still want us to go to your place?" Asks Brian

"Not anymore, I just want to spend time with you. Let us go park somewhere quiet. I have something to tell you". Said Laura

"Are you sure, I need to hear about it today? You have had a rough day already, let us do it when your head, mind and heart are all agreed. What about tomorrow?" Brian suggested.

She agreed and told him she was feeling emotionally drained and think some rest would probably rejuvenate her body. Laura hoped that Brian would invite her to his place instead; he just drove her back to her house. When Laura suggested he come in, he declines but promises to come the next day. Brian gave Laura a peck on the chin and a kiss on her forehead and said his bye.

Laura finds herself in a state of confusion. What is happening to her? Does Brian know what he is doing to her and does he really like her or is just faking it? She thought of many things, the life she had lived in shelters not knowing where her next meal would come from. She was always uncertain and wondered if anybody cared if she was dead or alive. With the exception of Tony (who occasionally helped her and protected her from sex scavengers), men who looked at her as if she was a piece of meat to be devoured at their convenience. Although she considered Brian different, he was still a man capable of hurting her with no notice. She need to be careful with him too, she warns herself as she enters her house.

CHAPTER 4

After dropping Laura at her place, Brian drives to his wife's grave to have a chat with her about Laura. He needed Hellen to understand how life had been unbearable without her and their daughter. He did not want to continue drowning in sorrow forever and needed her release. He talked to her about Laura, how sweet she was, and how she was making him want to live again. He promised Hellen, he would never forget them and would honor their memory as long as he lived. He leaves the graveside and on his way home, places a call to Laura. He was checking to see how she was doing and if she needed anything.

Laura hears the phone ring, checks the caller's identity and ignores it. With tears streaming down her face, she continues with her slow dance to her favorite reggae tune coming from her music box. Her room is now filling up fast with smoke from the joint she was puffing. She is trying to numb her sorrow and pain. Now she is considering ending her life to be at peace.

"For how long will I continue to feel this way?" She asks herself.

Laura hears a knock at her door and the door opens. She turns around, and sees Brian standing by the door looking concerned. She puts off her music, tries to wipe away her tears hoping he had not notice but it was too late. He moved swiftly towards her, pulled her gently towards him to comfort her. He holds her tightly to his body without saying a word. Laura burst out crying and sobs for close to five minutes in his arms. When she was done, he reassures her that things would be okay going forward. They sit down on the sofa as Brian wipes away her tears with the white handkerchief from his pocket.

"Why did you come back?" she asks him.

"I was worried about you, especially when you refused to pick up my call" He replied.

"Is that all?" Laura enquired.

"No, that is not all, I also realized I wanted to be with you and tell you something. I am sorry I was insensitive to your needs earlier, when you told me you had something to tell me. I should have listened. I ask for your forgiveness," Brian says

'I forgive you," Laura tells him as she leans forward touching his forehead gently.

"Will it be okay to open the door and windows for a few minutes? I will soon be drowning or choking from the smoke in this room," says Brian.

"Sure! I am sorry, I should have opened them, the moment you came, but I am glad you had enough time to inhale some of the good stuff you have been missing." Laura said teasingly.

They laughed while Laura opened the windows and door to have fresh air in the room. She comes back and settles in, right next to him on the sofa.

"So what did you want to tell me? You better start with the ring you are wearing." Said Laura.

"I will, but I do not want to be a bully by jumping the queue, you see, you were first in line and I cannot just swat your number away. Therefore, you need to go first." Responds Brian

"Is that out of consideration or just plain chickening out?" asks Laura

"No, it is out of concern and being a feminist it won't be fair for me to crash the party just because I am a man. You *had something to tell and you made it known earlier on. Therefore, I am going to respect that." Brian said*

Laura accepted his reasoning but with a caveat that he would go first next time they come to an impasse. Brian had no choice but agree. Laura goes into the kitchen to get coffee, which had been brewing. She brought Brian a mug and a cup for herself, and sat down. She told Brian she wanted him to know who she was and requested that he not judge her harshly. She informed him that he was the only person ever she is talking to about her life. Brian sat very quietly listening to every word from her mouth and showing he was listening by nodding. Laura felt at ease and started telling Brian about her childhood. She narrated how she missed her father who died just before she turned eight. How everything changed from then and got worse, the moment her mother remarried. How Mike never seem to appreciate anything she did, in spite of her good grades. Mike would always find fault with everything she did. She told him how her life changed completely when she turned fourteen that was when Mike started being violent and abusive to her mother and extending it to her. The violence started after he lost his job as a janitor at the neighborhood high school for exposing himself to a thirteen-year-old female student. Mike's response to his problems was to resort to heavy drinking and coming back home in the wee hours of the night every day.

"On the night of the worst abuse; I was asleep when he came into my room. I cannot remember anything else and I have tried to, ever since. Nevertheless, all I get are severe pains in my head each time I try. How I wish I can remember, why can't I remember?"

Brian began to understand how desperate Laura was. He reaches out to her and holds her. He continues to reassure her that it was going to be okay. He made the point that she did not have to force anything, it would come out in due time and at its own choosing whenever her mind was ready. He suggested that they end the conversation, as she appeared emotionally drained. Laura insists on continuing with her story, unless Brian was bored with it.

Brian had to tread carefully now; his professionalism and Laura's need to go on talking; began to weigh on his mind. He agreed he would continue listening on the condition that Laura would only talk about the things she could remember. He assured her that he would help her fill the blank parts of her memory later. Laura accepted his terms and the conversation resumed.

Laura told Brian what she remembers clearly about that morning was her mother taking away the blood stained sheets from her bed. She remember her mother yelling at her and blaming her for something, she could not remember what it was. The picture of her soaked pajamas in a mixture of blood and some white stuff is still stuck in her head. She also remember the excoriating pains in her private parts and the isolation she felt in the days that followed. She had asked her mother to take her to the hospital or to the police to press charges but she kept on bringing excuses for Mike. It was then that she realized she was alone with no protection in her own home. Soon afterward, the nightmares started. She told her mother about it but she did nothing.

"I had no choice but to run away from her and Mike. I do not regret it and I do not want to see them in my life." Laura says with some finality.

Brian leaned and moved closer to her, took her in his arms and cuddled her for a long time without talking. He could see how fate had brought them together to mend each other's broken hearts. Who would have imagined that accidental crash, which now appear to be unforgettable, could be responsible for fusing both their lives together?

There and then, like an epiphany, Brian knew he was in love with Laura. He would take care of her no matter the cost.

Laura on her part expected Brian to pull away or show aloofness of some sort; instead, he was holding her tightly as if he was afraid she would fly away. She knew then and at that moment that she wanted him in her life and was in love with him. The only thing stopping her from telling him about her feelings was the ring; he was wearing and perhaps the bad news he had, which he wanted to tell her. She was just about to scream out her frustrations, suddenly Brian kissed her and she simply melted away. The electric bolt she had felt, when they kissed the first time, was back and this time she was determined to follow its path to its end. She kissed Brian back with such passion and ferocity like one famished. Brian reciprocated with free flowing passion that took him by surprise as well. He kissed Laura slowly, deliberately and with such gentleness, which only helped open up more of Laura's lantern energy; that went on and on, building up a crescendo of mindlessness.

Just as suddenly, as he had started kissing her, Brian stopped. Laura looked at him questioningly and he shook his head. She could see the desire on his face and his struggle to contain it. Her heart melts from a warmth she has never felt before. Most of the men she has known would never come this close to being physically intimate with her and withdraw. Rather, they would force themselves on her whether she wanted it or not. Brian holds her by the hand and leads her to the couch. They sit down and he pulls her to him, placing her head on his chest. She hears his heart beat. It is beating so fast; she is afraid it would burst out from his chest.

Some minutes have passed now; she feels his heart beat slowing down. He keeps on holding her. She loves the feeling of her head on his chest. For some reason, she feels safe. She has never felt this way with any man before. Unconsciously she feels breath leave her mouth as she exhales. It is then that she realizes that she had been holding her breath. She begins to feel drowsy and slowly falls asleep.

Laura wakes up from her nap and for a moment has no clue, where she is. Then she hears the heart beat and it all comes back to her. She raises her head and notices that Brian had fallen asleep too. She takes this opportunity to look at his face critically. Laura notices the tired lines on top of Brian's lips and realizes they are the reason he looked older than 33 years. The bags under his eyes are not very obvious, but they are there. On his face is a combination of hardness and softness and she wonders what pain or secrets lurks underneath. As she continues to examine his face, it suddenly hits her, she is beginning to fall deeply in love with this man and she barely knows him! She is carried away, startled by the realization of her feelings for Brian, she does not notice that he is awake and is also looking at her through the slits in his eyes. When their eyes meet, he smiles and almost immediately a sad look flashes across his face. Brian starts apologizing to Laura.

"Forgive me for almost letting myself go" he starts.

"Sh! Sh! Sh!" Laura says as she tries to put a finger across his lips.

He gently pushes her finger away and continues.

"No, I need to say this. It is important that we start this relationship on a solid foundation. And to do that, I need to be cognizant at all times of my responsibilities". He insists.

He goes on to tell her, that there is so much they need to know about each other and it is important to take the time to build a relationship that would last and not allow themselves to be carried away by the heat of the moment. Laura agrees with him but at the same time wonder, what it all means. Whatever it meant, she loved it. The feeling of not having the need to do anything to be accepted, the feeling of not being rushed into anything, the feeling that everything is finally going to be okay. He pulls her head back unto his chest and they lie back on the couch.

After they had rested, they decided to go out for dinner at one of the finest restaurants in town. However, that would be after they have gone over to Brian's to freshen up. On the way to Brian's they had a detour to a boutique. Brian went into the boutique while Laura waited in the car. He comes out, almost immediately, holding a bag in his hand. When they arrived at Brian's, he gives Laura a tour of the house and hands her clean towels and showed her the bathroom. Brian excused himself to go look for fresh clothes to wear for the evening date. In the bathroom, Laura fills up the tub with hot water. She finds a bottle of bubble bath liquid, she pours a considerable amount of the liquid into the water, and she goes in.

Laura finds the water warm and soothing. As she washes her skin with the washcloth, she can almost feel all the dirt unassociated with her skin cleansed away. It is a good feeling, one she never thought she would experience.

Brian started to fear they would be late for their dinner reservation so he reluctantly went into the bathroom to remind Laura they were running out of time. He informed her of a bag on the bed waiting for her attention. He then left the room to give her time to dress. Laura saw the bag, as soon as she entered the bedroom. She opened it and found a note instructing her, to put on everything she saw in the bag. She started by drying her hair with the blow dryer she found in the room, put on some makeup and got dressed. She was impressed that the leather shoes, a gold necklace, a wristwatch, a leather belt, and the dress in the bag fit her perfectly. The surprise was not finished. Right next to the bag was a single red rose flower, and a note that simply said, "I know it is not February, but will you be my forever valentine?"

Laura was so touched and overwhelmed, by so much emotion that she cried. She was happy and at the same time sad. All her life, the only person she could remember, buying her anything new and of value was her late father. Now here is a man that she did not know two weeks ago, doing this and other things for her. "What did I do to deserve this man?" she asks herself loudly.

Brian walks into the bedroom and finds her in deep thoughts. She wipes her tears with the back of her hand and asks Brian if he loves her or just likes her. Brian tries to avoid the question and suggests that they take a moment to think everything through things because they cannot afford to be flippant in the things they say to each other. They both agree to focus on what is at hand and revisit the matter at an appropriate time.

"Brian, I know we both agreed to do this and let me also say how grateful I am for your gifts but I cannot accept them until what I have asked for has been settled. I refuse to be a charity case." Laura says

"Sweetie, you are being difficult on this issue, I understand how you feel but remember this was meant to be a celebration for our coming together in a very special way. Our being together means so much to me, and I want to think it does as well for you. Please let us enjoy our time together and make the evening a special one. The hotel we are going to requires that we appear in a certain way and that is the reason I took the initiative to do this. I wanted to make it a surprise." Brian begs

"I do not mean to sound un-appreciative, and I suppose you went through all this because you care. You know, that

is the reason I asked the question in the first place. I wanted to know the extent of your feelings for me," Said Laura

"We are saying the same thing, only in a different way. Let us walk this path together, starting with the dinner. It will be a privilege tonight to walk hand in hand into the hotel in the company of the most gorgeous woman I know. I cannot wait to see the heads turn as I walk in with you. It would be to my uttermost pleasure, to see you wear that dress; I know it will look great on you." Brian said

"Oh! Brian, you always know what to say to me. Why do I fall for every trick that come out of your mouth? It is very hard to say no to you. Tell me, have you charmed me?" asks Laura

"I will let you in on the secret if you finish dressing up." He said

"Ok, for your sake I will." Laura finally acquiesced to Brian.

Brian moved deeper into his wardrobe and grabbed a black suit, a blue shirt, a leather belt and black leather shoes. Laura helped him get his underwear from the drawers. Laura on her part only needed to put the final touches on her face. She was ready in just a few minutes. Looking at her, Brian notices that the dress on her body is like a second skin, draping her curves and swishing gently around her legs. She looked so beautiful and vibrant. He wondered how the streets could have hidden and denied the world the opportunity to appreciate such beauty in a woman.

Laura looked so comfortable in her skin. With a height close to six foot, golden curled hair, rapture -blue eyes, sharp cute nose, defined lips, and long neck. Laura pleasing facial appearance was hard to miss. However, she could not hide her appreciation of Brian's bold attempt to change her looks and perception of self. She was pleased with how Brian looked and felt drawn to him even more.

"I must say this at the onset. Sweetie, you look stunning, so beautiful in your dress beyond my wildest imagination. I thought you were beautiful, but I am changing my mind on that; beautiful does not give you the right classification. You are simply gorgeous and I am privileged to have you." Brian said with so much warmth.

"You mean that? "Thank you so much dear for turning me into a believer. Who in their right mind would have thought that a street woman like me would be wearing such expensive clothes, looking beautiful and feeling magnificently joyful?" Laura spoke with such enthusiasm.

"I mean every word I am saying to you." Brian spoke from the heart.

"Thank you so very much once again. I believe in you Brian." Laura said, with a heart-felt appreciation

"You are welcome," says Brian

They both knew they were running late for their dinner appointment and need to leave the house immediately. Brian had booked a table at the luxurious Mayfair Hotel in down town by the beachfront. The establishment have a reputation for being strict with scheduled appointments.

"We will go in the convertible," says Brian. Referring to the Mercedes Benz that belonged to his late wife Hellen. Laura goes out of the house ahead of Brian and gets into the car. When he emerges, Brian jump into the car and speeds away. He gets them to the hotel just at the nick of time.

CHAPTER 5

As Laura stepped into the lobby of the hotel, she gasps for air. She has never seen such beauty and majestic exhibition of opulence within a building anywhere. Everything before her appeared perfect and exquisitely arranged to detail. The serenity and ambiance of the whole place would knock anyone's breath away. She held onto Brian's hand, as they walked in and they could not help but notice heads turning to watch them. Laura obviously is an instant hit. She and her dress was something to gawk at. Brian could not have been more proud of her. He takes advantage of their five minutes of fame by holding her hand tightly as well, smiling and nodding his head at anyone who looked in their direction. They arrive at the reservation desk and as the waiter guides them to their table, most people in the restaurant nod in their direction as they walk to their seats. Brian waves at them and takes a bow while Laura stands by his side smiling shyly astonished at the attention they are receiving. Brian pulls out a chair for Laura and then takes his own seat.

A second waiter comes to take their orders. First, they order for appetizers and drinks and subsequently for the main course. As they waited for their appetizers and drinks, they chattered. Mainly focusing on the events of the past hours. Laura was inquisitive and wanted to know if Brian could explain to her what love; truly is. She told him, she would not know how to differentiate it from clichés.

Brian started by telling her, that everything she wants to know has both a positive and a negative aspect to it. That love in itself has its origin: from the maker of life.

"What do you mean from the maker of life?" Laura asked

"Well, let me start this from the beginning of time, because that is where it originates. I know this is not the right place or time to talk about this; however, you have asked and I will briefly give you the synopsis of what I have come to believe.

You see the purpose of man when God created him, was supposed to be for relational – fellowship. Inside his soul, He equipped him with functions that would always crave for nearness with respect to their fellowship together. When man rebelled, that harmonious, perfect relationship was cut off, but the functions that He had placed in His creation remained in humanity. To this day, every human being craves to fill that perfect, harmonious presence with something, in trying to restore that lost relational." Brian stated

"I am getting lost in all this, it is new to me" says Laura

"Remember I told you earlier, this is not the right place for this discussion," Brian added

"Yes! You did but just before we suspend it, how does love come into this?" Asks Laura

"Do you agree that the greatest desire, which everyone has, is to love or be loved?" Asks Brian

"It is true, that is the most sort after condition by everyone. What does it mean then?" Laura asked

"It means to feel fulfilled. We all seek to fill the void within our soul with love. It is the lost relational togetherness with our creator, which in essence is what we are all searching. This ultimately means God is Love. Let's talk some more if you want, when we get home, if that is that okay?" Brian says to Laura

"Yes dear! I want to hear some more. I need to understand why it is painful when you do not feel loved." Laura says with some sadness.

Their first course arrived as Laura was finishing her statement. Brian reached out to her, took her hand with both of his hands; kissed it and asked the waiter if he could bring her single rose flower. The waiter obliged and was back after a few minutes. He then presented the flower proclaiming to her "I love you Laura."

Laura was touched and moved, got up from her chair and planted a deep kiss on Brian's lips that seemed to last forever. When they came up for air, a whole section of patrons close-by started clapping for them, especially the women. Laura went back to her seat a bit embarrassed by the attention she had drawn to themselves. She quietly seeped her drink and helped herself to the appetizer on her plate. Brian on the other hand was enjoying every bit of it and seemed so pleased with himself.

Laura looks at him and exclaims, "You set me up, Mr. Romantic!"

They continued with the appetizers and drinks, until their meal arrived. They ate, chatted and drank some more wine. With their dinner completed, they retreated to the patio outside facing the ocean to have their dessert. Laura excused herself to visit the washroom for some padding while Brian sat there with a beam on his face but also lost in thought. He remembered how the budding romance started and how he almost missed it all by not taking a chance. He was glad he did. He looked up and saw Laura coming, as she crossed the main dining area to get to him, the chilly ocean breeze made her dress move as if it was alive, and she swiped at the golden hair blinding her. She looked stunningly gorgeous, radiant, sexy and vivacious at the same time. He was glad he was with such a woman.

Laura went straight for the yoghurt covered frozen strawberries she had ordered for dessert as if it would disappear if she did not eat it right then. Brian had ice cream and coffee. They chatted some more over their past and the challenges that they have had.

"I hope someday you will tell me, how it has been for you, and how you arrived here. Especially your transition to street life." Brian stated

"Sure anytime." Says Laura

"Remember a while ago in the dining room, when I gave you the rose and you had a standing ovation? I said something to you, just before you kissed me. Do you remember what it was?" He asked

She hesitated for a while and then remembered. "Oh! Yes, you said you love me. I am sorry I did not get a chance to say it back. That is what I was saying with the kiss though. Brian, I have been in love with you since the day you brought "Lilly" back. However, if you want to hear it loud and clear. Yes, I will say it. I love you too." She pronounced emphatically. Moreover, if I cannot love you, I wonder what kind of a person my heart would find acceptable."

"Thank you Laura." He says.

"You are welcome, and now that I know how you feel about me, would it be proper to call you, my love, if I choose to do so?" She asks

"You can call me anything you want, as long as it is coming from your heart and the truth," Brian told her

> *Shortly after, they asked for, paid their bill, and left for Brian's Place. Brian drove into the garage and used the access door from there to gain entry into the main house. Laura headed straight into the washroom to relieve herself, while Brian went to the kitchen to get some refreshments. He came out of the kitchen holding two glasses of wine. One for Laura and the other for himself. Laura was already sitting at the table close to the bedroom door as Brian joined her. They sat, chatted and drank their wine. Laura stood up to go look at the frames of pictures on the wall. As she walked from one picture to the other, his eyes followed her movements. Looking at her with the way her dress wrapped*

around her body showing her contours made his heart start to beat as he felt stirrings of desire. He stood up and walked to her. She was engrossed at the picture of Brian and Hellen; she did not notice he was standing right behind her. He gently put his arms around her waist, pressing himself tightly against her body. Laura gasps and turns to face him. She sees the intensity of his desire in his eyes, and she shivers. Without hesitation, she starts unbuttoning his shirt as his fingers, traced a warm tingly path, on the back of her dress. She traces his lips with a finger and gives out a soft moan as she kissed him. Brian lifts her legs one after the other wraps them round his body. He turns to go into the bedroom, then he stops, take a deep breath and tell Laura he has something he wants to tell her.

"Please do not stop, I can still hear it through all this, I beg of you," Laura pleads

"Please! Laura, hear me out. At this very moment, believe me; I am struggling to hold it together. I am going to need your help with this. We cannot allow our passions get the better of us. There is a line, which we cannot cross at this stage in our relationship and I ask that you hold me accountable, each time I try to cross that line. See, everything in me wants you so badly, however I must do

what is right by you and us. I want us to be intimately together both spiritually and physically. What I was about to do was physical but the spiritual aspect of it is missing and that is what we must fix before we move further. I know how hurtful this sounds right now but I truly believe one day we shall be thankful that we waited to do it right. I truly apologize for starting it and allowing my weakness to cause so much pain to you." He tells her

"I need to rest my head, it's like I am falling. Can I rest on the bed?" she asked

"Sure" Brian said as he took her to the bedroom and gently lay her on the bed. "Sweetie, do you want me to go and let you rest?"

"No, no! Protested Laura. Stay and talk to me. Is this what love is, does doing it right means this pain and why does it hurt this badly?"

"I am sorry you are hurting and I am very to blame for that. Once again, forgive me, but to answer your question: It hurts badly because our heart is seeking for the rightful solution to cure the absence therein and more often, it matters less whether the cure is temporary or permanent as long as it is a fix. Right now, the pain comes from longing for the love that it feels it is not permitted. You asked what

love is: It bears all things, believes all things, hopes all things, and endures all things"

"I am glad I met you, regardless of how everything turns out. You are one in all and what a privilege it was to crash into you with my shopping cart that day. The unforgettable crash that is slowly mending my heart," said Laura with so much satisfaction. One more thing she adds, "Would it be too much if I spend this night with you here at your place? We do not need to do anything more but talk, as hard as it may get; I promise I will not cross the line"

Brian just smiled feeling so relieved to have a woman who could speak her mind quite freely. He loved her the more for that.

"Sweetie, I love you for saying and speaking your mind on that. I wanted to ask you myself but I guess you have beaten me to the punch. I would truly love it if you could spend the night here with me. It would give me a chance to share some things with you that you need to know." Brian tells her. They both refreshed themselves, and changed into comfortable clothes for the night.

As soon as they got into bed, Brian started to talk about Hellen and his daughter and the pain of losing them. He blamed himself for the accident that claimed their lives.

He was supposed to have picked Janet from her school but because he was running late for a meeting, Hellen went to pick her up instead and that was when the accident happened. Laura tried to comfort him by assuring him that it was not his fault. That things happen and most of the time, circumstances are beyond our control.

He looks at her thoughtfully and smiles. "I don't know why I am still seeing Dr. Sullivan for my sessions, you are just as good as a counsellor, you know" Brian says.

You see, having you as a counsellor would be getting two for the price of one. Not only will I have you, but also I will save money given that my payment to you will be in kind. My payment will be in the form of cooking, giving you baths and running your errands. What do you think, is that a good deal or what?" He asks.

"I will have to consider it but if you add having my monthly menstrual periods on my behalf, it will be a deal," She retorts. They burst out laughing and just wished nights like this would be the norm.

Laura, tells him about Anthony. How he made himself her guardian from age sixteen and tried his best to protect her from men who always wanted to take advantage of her. She told him about Tony's friend John, who took advantage of his absence one day and sexually assaulted her. When Anthony got back and heard of it, he broke the man's jaw and sent him to the hospital for two months.

"I would like to meet this Anthony and thank him for looking after you, all those years," said Brian

"You have already met him. Do you remember the man you talked to when you first came looking for me. The guy who took your forty bucks and gave you no information?"

"Yes, I do. The Puerto Rican dude, was that him? By the way, he was the one who led me to you. I am therefore grateful he took my money. It was worth it," Brian said with a smile.

"Why on earth did I then think you hired some investigator who tracked me down? I was upset with you at first, thinking you had no business doing that, but when you handed me Lilly my heart felt so grateful." Says Laura

"You see after he took my money but gave me no information. I went and sat in my car, literally very angry with myself. He did not know where I parked and what my car looked like. As I sat there after a while, I saw the two of you emerge from an alley. You were pushing your cart and I followed you from a distance to your house." Brian informs her

"Oh! My goodness, I never knew that was how you found me," said Laura astonished

"Did you also know that I had an accident prior to meeting Tony, a few metres away from the location where you sculpt? I was looking for a spot to park, because I had just seen you sculpting while driving by. I forgot to check how the traffic, ahead of me was moving and ended up crashing into a car. By the time, I finished exchanging papers with the other driver, and went to look for you; you were gone. Madam, you have given me many headaches. At this time, I can only think of one thing as a repayment."

"What, let it not be what I am thinking?" said Laura

"A kiss would suffice; or would that be too much?" Brian asked

Oh! Darling, I will give you a thousand kisses for all your troubles, if that is what it takes. Please! I am sorry about your accident. Did you say you love me?" Laura asked very cheekily.

"I love you more now than I did two seconds ago." Brian told her with so much assurance in his voice.

After such an eventful day, and a beautiful evening, filled with good food, laughter and frank conversation they fell asleep in each other's arms. They woke up the next day a

Saturday at around 10am taking their time to get out of bed. Brian made breakfast and served it to Laura in bed. Laura was beside herself, happy and quite pleased with the top-notch service she was receiving. She planted a kiss on Brian's chin, held his head with her two hands, brought it close to her face and told him, that she loved him. With breakfast over, Laura suggested that Brian drops her at her place; she had some chores to attend.

They set out, and soon were at her place. As Brian pulled into the driveway of her house, he notices a tall, good-looking brown man sitting on the steps leading into the house. He obviously was waiting. Brian turns and looks at Laura questioningly and she whispers 'Tony'. Laura opens the door, gets out of the car, and starts to walk towards Anthony who was muttering to himself, he ignores her and goes straight for Brian who recognizes him as Anthony, the man who had swindled him of his hard-earned money. Tony turns around with an obvious change of mind and turns back towards Laura. When he got close to her, he lunged at Laura, holding her by the neck and demanded to know where she had been all night. Brian taken aback and sensing danger, tries to intervene by trying to stop Tony from choking Laura. Instead, he finds himself on the ground, bloodied and bleeding profusely from his nose and mouth. Tony had punched him so hard on his mouth, sending him reeling to the ground. Laura rushes over to Brian to try to save him from the brute while yelling at him to stop. Tony walks away promising he would kill Brian the next time he sees him with Laura.

"I am so sorry about all this. Let me get you something to stop the bleeding." Laura says as she leads Brian into her house. She gets a towel and a bowl of cold water and immediately goes to work, wiping the blood from his face while applying pressure to Brian's nose. The bleeding stopped after sometime and she concentrated on cleaning Brian up. She led him into a room, lay him down on the bed while continuing with her first aid and apologizing at every given chance.

"What was that? I thought you said he is just a mentor, is there something going on that I am missing?" Asks Brian.

"There is nothing going on. Since I was sixteen, Tony has always seen me as a child and thinks any man who even shows an appearance of interest or being close to me is an enemy and ought to be dealt with." Laura stated

"The way it looked, I do not think he sees you as just some woman. I think he is in love with you and it is something

69

you should deal with before somebody else gets seriously hurt. I also think he has mental issues and needs help." Brian says conclusively.

"What should I do? As much as I am grateful to him for taking me in, at a time when nobody cared whether I lived or died, I cannot live in fear thinking he is going to hurt someone on my account. I will not allow him to jeopardize my life or my affairs especially with those that I love. I care about him a lot. Not as anything but as a friend and a mentor who taught me how to survive the streets with my chin held high." Laura says pensively.

"I will see what to do to help him. I will make calls to the veteran affairs and see if he can receive help." Brian stated Laura thanked Brian for agreeing to help Tony with his mental condition. She looks at him realizing how she is in awe of him. How can he even think of helping someone who almost ended his life? She thought to herself as she pulls out a T-shirt from inside a drawer, for Brian, to wear. Brian's phone rings and it is Dr. Sullivan his counsellor, who wants to meet him on an urgent matter. He informs Laura that he had to go and meet with his shrink. Laura reluctantly lets him go, promising to call him later once she has had a talk with Anthony.

Brian drove from Laura's house to Dr. Sullivan apartment, which was located in the leafy suburbs of the city. Unbeknown to him, a car had followed him from the moment he left Laura's house. Whoever it was, also parked their car just across Brian's Toyota cruiser and waited for him. Dr. Sullivan offers him a glass of wine and notices Brian has swollen mouth and lips.

"You look messed up, what happened to you. Did a truck hit you?" Dr. Sullivan asked Brian

"It is a long story, but I did not come here to talk about me. What is so urgent that you dragged me away on my day off to come meet you?" asked Brian

"I cannot talk about it with you when you are in such a mess. I need to know what you are dealing with. Does it have to do with Hellen? I thought we had made so much progress in that area?" Dr. Sullivan quipped

"It has nothing to do with Hellen. I just ran into someone who decided to teach me some manners over a woman." Stated Brian

"I did not know you were seeing some woman. The only person I recall you mentioning to me lately was that trashy woman, the pot smoker, that rude woman ..." Brian sharply cut him off

"I will not allow you to continue disrespecting a woman I love in that manner. She is a very special woman. In addition, since Hellen, she is the only woman who has given me sanity. I love her and nothing you say is going to change that. You focus on class difference, does it matter if she is an artist and I am a CEO of a company? What is important is the connection between two people not the class they belong. In fact, you have known of the mountains I had to climb and the agony I have suffered because of Hellen's death and that of my daughter. You should be the first to congratulate me for finding someone who can help me recalibrate my life back to normalcy. She makes me exceedingly happy, and I pray I do the same for her. If the world cannot accept that, then they can all go into the abyss for all I care." Brian picked up his car keys and left in a huff without waiting to find out why the doctor had summoned him in the first place. He got into the car and sped away towards the city center. As he drove, he opened his glove compartment to look for his anti - anxiety bottle of pills and found none. Since he was too anxious, he thought he could find relief by talking to someone who would understand his condition. One who will not judge him by the choices he had made. He raced towards Hellen's

graveside hoping to convey to her his frustrations with her brother over the issue with Laura. All along, the car with its unknown occupants was also busy following his every step at a few metres distance, bidding their time to carry out their heinous, nefarious plot.